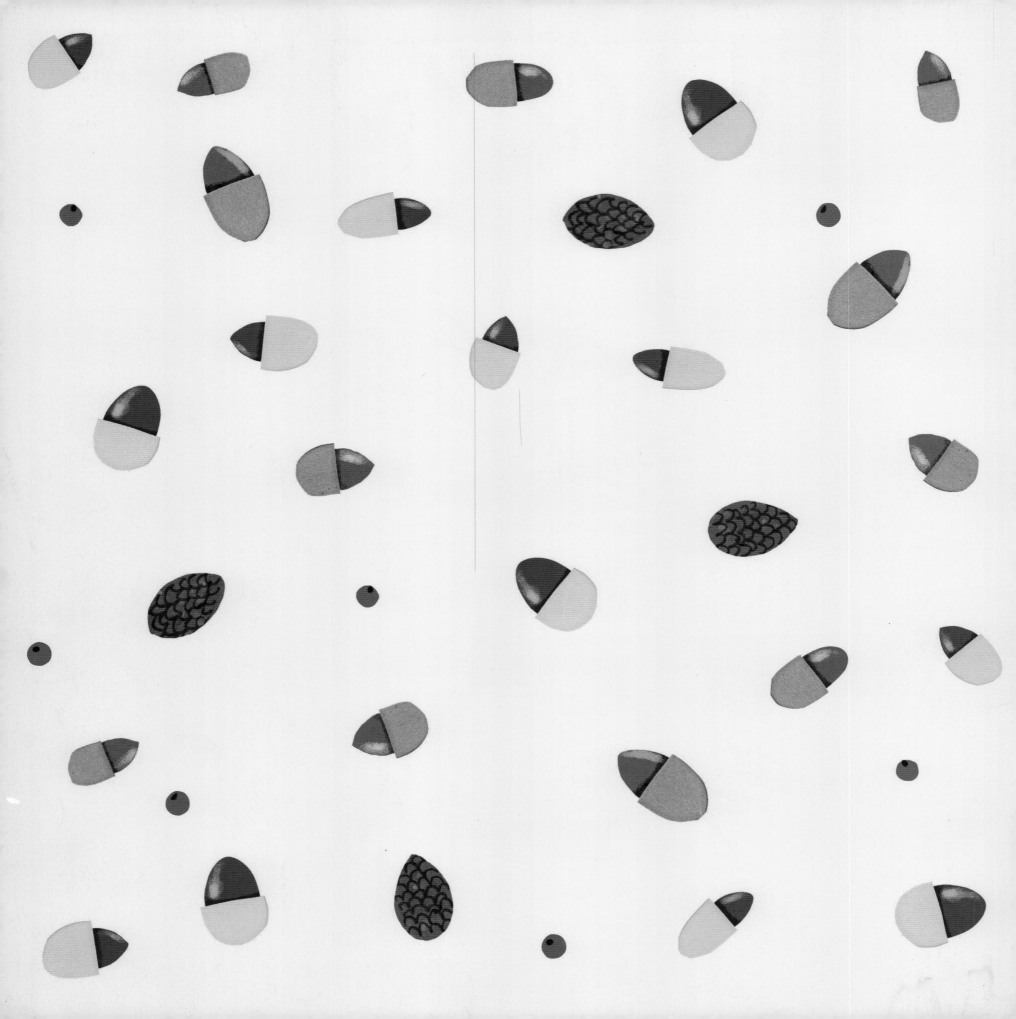

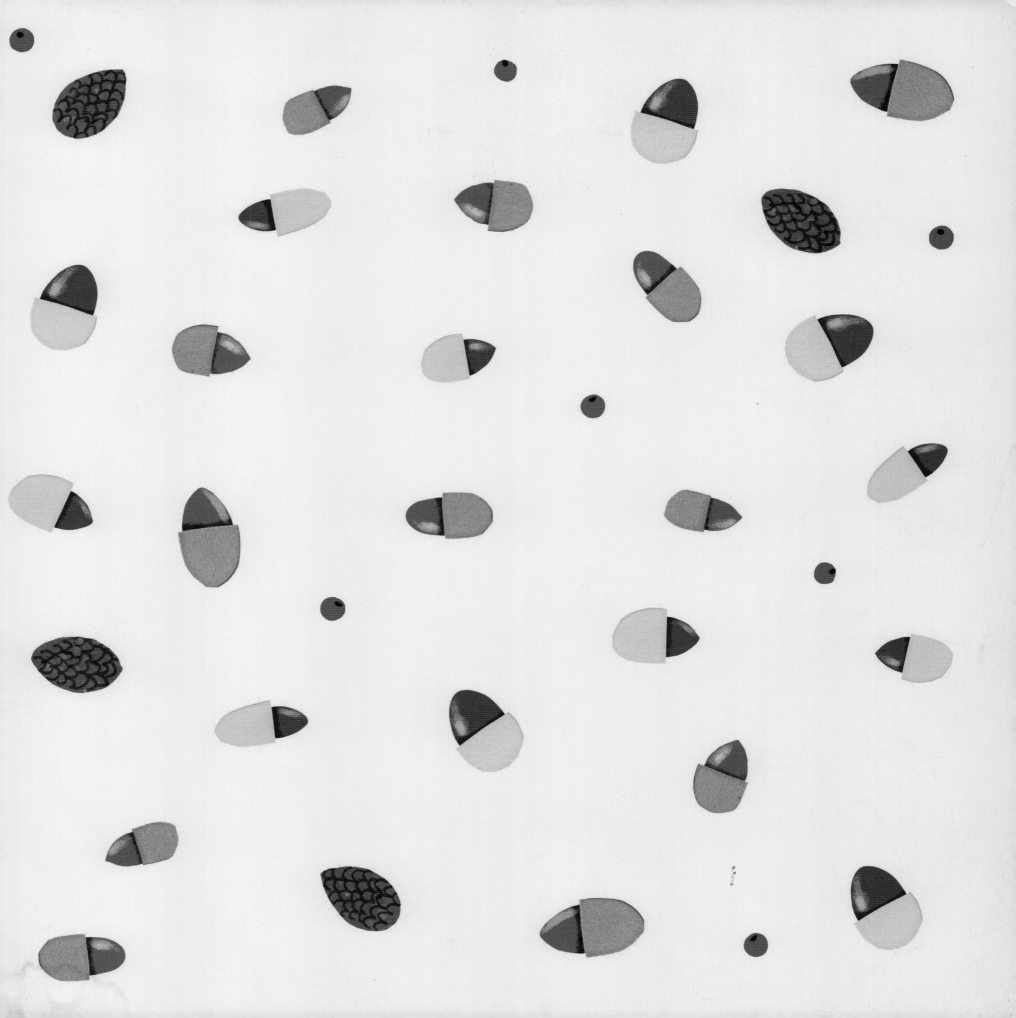

For Dashura Ariana xx
P.M.

For Christian and Helen, with love
C.J-I.

First published 2013 by Macmillan Children's Books
This edition published 2014 by Macmillan Children's Books
a division of Macmillan Publishers Limited
20 New Wharf Road, London N1 9RR
Basingstoke and Oxford
Associated companies throughout the world
www.panmacmillan.com

ISBN: 978-1-4472-8155-9

Text copyright © Paula Metcalf 2013
Illustrations copyright © Cally Johnson-Isaacs 2013
Moral rights asserted.

3 5 7 9 8 6 4 2

A CIP catalogue record for this book is available from the British Library.

Printed in China

Charlie Crow in the Snow

Written by
Paula Metcalf

Illustrated by
Cally Johnson-Isaacs

MACMILLAN CHILDREN'S BOOKS

At the top of a grassy hill, overlooking a stream, stood Charlie's tree.

He was so proud of his magnificent home!

Sometimes Bear and Swallow came to visit,
and they told stories and watched the sun set.
Charlie felt like the happiest crow alive!

But all of that was before the
strange happenings started . . .

First the sun disappeared, leaving the sky grey and cold. "Maybe it's staying in bed," thought Charlie.

A few days later, the leaves on his tree started to flutter away. "Stop! Come back!" he squawked.

And when Charlie went for his Sunday bath,
he got the biggest surprise of all . . .

Somebody had turned
the water to GLASS!

Poor Charlie, how confusing it all was!
"Bear and Swallow will know what's going on,"
he thought. And he hopped off to find them.

But all around was oddly quiet.

Charlie was just about to give up his search when he bumped into a squirrel. She looked confused too!

"Have you noticed all these strange happenings?" she whimpered.

Charlie nodded. "Whatever next?" he asked worriedly.

They didn't have to wait long to find out. Moments later, white flakes started floating down from the sky.

"Oh dear!" exclaimed Charlie, "these look like bits of cloud!"

"But clouds belong in the sky!" cried Squirrel. "Next it'll be the stars . . ."

"And maybe even the MOON will fall down!" she shrieked.

Suddenly, her squealing was interrupted by a deep, growly voice . . .

"Keep it down out there," the voice said. "Some of us are trying to sleep!"

"There you are, Bear!" exclaimed Charlie. "Help us!
The clouds are falling down and the water has turned to glass!"

"Oh Charlie!" laughed Bear. "It's not glass, it's ice!"
He told them all about the cold winter, when swallows fly far
away to the sunshine and bears stay in bed to keep warm.

Charlie and Squirrel peered into
Bear's den. It looked so cosy!
"You're very welcome to join
me for a snooze," he said.
"Ooh, thanks Bear!"
squeaked Squirrel.
And in they went.

Charlie and Squirrel concentrated hard on falling asleep, but . . .

"These leaves are so itchy!" whispered Charlie, having a scratch.

Squirrel tossed and turned. "I just can't sleep," she sighed.
"Singing can help," said Charlie, and he started humming. Squirrel joined in.

They were just about to reach the chorus when Bear sat bolt upright . . .

"ENOUGH! Bears need their sleep," he boomed. "You two fidgety fleas will have to go. SHOO!"

Back outside in the cold, Squirrel's teeth started chattering.
"Wh . . . wh . . . what now?" she asked.

"Well," said Charlie, "if we can't sleep through winter, let's fly away like Swallow!"

At Charlie's tree, Squirrel was in charge of packing for the journey.
"Just a snack or two to keep us going," she said.

Charlie steadied himself for take-off, then took an enormous leap.

"SUNSHINE HERE WE COME!" he squawked.

But it wasn't so easy flying
with a passenger!

"Oh dear!" cried Charlie.

"Oh no!" cried Squirrel.

"OH HELP!"
they both cried together.

They closed their eyes and
waited for the crash-landing . . .

But instead they landed FLUUUMPHH! in a soft, snowy heap.

"THAT," said Squirrel breathlessly, "was the most fun EVER!"

And they soon discovered there was plenty more fun to be had in the snow.

"Isn't winter perfect?" laughed Squirrel.

"Oh yes!" Charlie agreed. "Although I wish Bear and Swallow were with us."

Then a lovely idea crept into Squirrel's mind.

"Er, Charlie," she said, "all this fun
has made me VERY hungry. I'm going
to go and get us a snack."

Squirrel was gone for a long time. "Where IS she?" Charlie wondered.

His tummy was starting to rumble, so he hopped up the hill to find her.

When Charlie reached his tree, Squirrel was not on her own!

"Surprise!" giggled Squirrel. "I made them just for you, Charlie. They'll keep us company until the real Bear and Swallow come back!"

"Oh Squirrel," said Charlie, "thank you! What a lovely thing to do."

Snow Bear and Snow Swallow didn't say much, but that didn't matter.

As Charlie and Squirrel watched the snow glowing pinkly under the setting sun . . .

Charlie, once again, felt like the happiest crow alive.